A Pedlar

Market Hall at Ledbury

...maid

A Travelling Coach

An Armed Merchantman

Puritans

Series 561

Here is the story of an important figure in English history, a brave and deeply-religious man who was a friend of all honest men—and who fought for many years against what he believed to be tyranny and injustice.

Helen

Francis

OLIVER CROMWELL

by L. DU GARDE PEACH,
M.A., Ph.D., D.Litt.

with illustrations
by JOHN KENNEY

Publishers : Ladybird Books Ltd . Loughborough
© Ladybird Books Ltd (formerly Wills & Hepworth Ltd) 1963
Printed in England

OLIVER CROMWELL

Oliver Cromwell is one of the most important figures in English history. In the time in which he lived, a great man was needed to lead the people of England in their fight for freedom, and to-day we still enjoy freedoms which he won for us.

Cromwell was born at Huntingdon in the year 1599, and it was on a large farm that he grew up. One story tells of an adventure which happened to him whilst he was staying at the house of his grandfather, Sir Henry Cromwell.

Sir Henry had a pet monkey which was allowed to climb all over the house, and one day it seized hold of Oliver, who was only a few months old, and carried him up on to the roof.

We can imagine the horror with which his grandfather must have seen the monkey climbing about the roof with the baby in its arms. But it is impossible to imagine what England might have been like to-day if the monkey had dropped him.

4

0 7214 0173 2

Oliver had six sisters but no brothers, so his friends were the boys of the little town, who were his schoolmates. We do not know whether this future ruler of England was a good scholar, but there are many stories to show that he was much like other boys.

Oliver's uncle, Sir Oliver Cromwell, was an important man, and lived on an estate much larger than the farm belonging to Oliver's father. He was in fact so important in the county that on more than one occasion he was visited by the King, James I.

On one of these visits the King was accompanied by his son Charles, and whilst Sir Oliver was entertaining the King, the two boys, Oliver Cromwell and Prince Charles, were sent into the garden to play. According to the story, the boys quarrelled and fought, and Oliver was the winner.

Years later they were to fight again, each with an army at his back, and happily for England, it was again Cromwell who was to be victorious.

When he was seventeen years of age Cromwell entered the University of Cambridge.

In the Middle Ages few people in England except the monks could read or write. Even kings and great nobles could often only just manage to write their names. Then, about the time of Edward I, who was the King of England from 1272 to 1307, rich men began to found schools and colleges up and down the country. Many grammar schools, and most of the colleges of Oxford and Cambridge Universities, were founded during the next two or three hundred years. The famous school of Eton dates from 1400.

At first intended for poor boys, these schools and universities were soon filled with the sons of rich merchants, and by Cromwell's time it was not easy for a poor boy to get into any one of them.

Shakespeare, who went to a grammar school in Stratford-on-Avon, writes about the schoolboy "with shining morning face, creeping like a snail unwillingly to school." As schools often started at six o'clock in the morning, it is not surprising that school-boys were unwilling in those days !

Cromwell remained less than a year at Cambridge. When his father died he had to return to Huntingdon to look after the farm. Soon after this he went to London for a while to study law, and whilst there he married the daughter of Sir James Bouchier, a rich London merchant.

It is sixty-two miles from London to Huntingdon. Oliver Cromwell and his wife would probably spend two days on the journey, travelling in a coach over roads little better than rough tracks.

A royal duke who visited England just before Oliver Cromwell was born, wrote of a journey from London to Cambridge: "On the road we passed through a villainous boggy and wild country, where the mud was so deep that it would scarcely be possible to pass with a coach in rainy weather."

If they spent a night on the way, they would stay at an inn, where they would find good food and lodging for two or three shillings. Although the English roads were bad, English inns were at that time among the best in the world.

The estate, really a large farm, to which Cromwell and his wife returned, supplied most of their needs. A writer called Sir Thomas Overbury, who lived at the same time as Cromwell, described the life on just such a farm. "His own farm yields him both food and raiment, and he is pleased with any nourishment God sends."

Because Cromwell was not a poor man, he could in addition buy linen for the house and silks and laces for his wife, and such things as sugar and spices, which could not be grown on the farm.

It was a healthy, open-air life which Cromwell lived for the next twenty years. He rose early because he believed that too much sleep is a bad habit. He worked in the fields with his farm servants, but he also took a lively interest in the affairs of the countryside, and in 1628 he was elected Member of Parliament for Huntingdon.

This was the beginning of the career which was to end as Lord Protector of England.

The Parliament to which Cromwell went in 1628 was a stormy one. King Charles I had been collecting taxes without the consent of the people, and had imprisoned a number of men for refusing to lend him money.

Parliament was determined that such illegal actions should be stopped, and a member of Parliament called Eliot drew up a list of complaints against the King. When it was put to the vote of the House of Commons the Speaker tried to prevent it being passed, because he was afraid of the King's anger. In the end he had to be held in his chair whilst the members voted. This was because no vote in the House of Commons is legal unless the Speaker is present.

The King immediately dissolved Parliament, and Cromwell returned to Huntingdon. He was now a changed man. He had spoken in Parliament and had shared the anger of the members at the illegal actions of the King.

It was to be eleven years before another Parliament met at Westminster. During that time many people grew to hate and distrust King Charles.

At this time there were in England a large number of people known as Puritans. We have come to think of these people as disliking any sort of happiness and always going about with gloomy faces, intent on preventing others from enjoying themselves. This is wrong. They were not *all* like that.

Oliver Cromwell was a Puritan, but he liked music and dancing and was fond of going to horse races. There were many like him.

The first people to be called Puritans lived in the time of Elizabeth. The name was given to them because they wanted to 'purify' the services and government of the Church by making them very much simpler. When James I followed Elizabeth, he demanded that all Puritans be driven out of the country.

Because there were so many of them this was impossible, and soon they were joined by many more who disliked the way in which King Charles was governing the country. It was only those who thought that everyone was wicked except themselves, and that to be good you had to be gloomy, who got the Puritans a bad name.

If we had lived in England in Cromwell's time we would have noticed that there was a wide difference between the clothes worn by the Puritans and those who were on the side of the King and the Church.

It was a time when wealthy people mostly dressed in coloured velvets and silks, with lace collars and cuffs, and rich embroidery on their coats and dresses. Many of the men wore lace or coloured ribbons at their knees, and all wore their hair very long. The King and his court must have been a very gay and colourful sight.

The Puritans did exactly the opposite. They wore simple clothes in dull colours, with plain white collars. The women wore dark dresses and no jewellery. What chiefly distinguished the Puritan men from the Royalists, as the King's men were called, was the fact that the Puritans cut their hair shorter. Because of this, they were later known as Roundheads.

The Puritans were quiet and sober in their speech and habits, and always strictly observed the Sabbath day.

Many things were happening in England during the eleven years of the King's government without a Parliament. Sir John Eliot, who had drawn up the list of grievances, was imprisoned and died in the Tower of London.

One of the things which made the people angry was a tax called Ship Money. In earlier days the towns on the coast of England had been forced to supply ships for the navy. This way of getting ships cost the King nothing, and it was now illegally revived. Some of the coastal towns, where there were no ships, were made to pay money instead, and soon every town in the country, whether it was on the coast or not, was ordered to contribute.

Many men refused to pay, amongst them John Hampden, a cousin of Oliver Cromwell.

Another brave Englishman, William Prynne, who had written against the illegal taxes, was made to stand in the pillory. Crowds of people gathered to show that they were on his side, and the King's Guard were unable to disperse them.

Whilst his cousin, John Hampden, was being tried for refusing to pay ship money, Oliver Cromwell was fighting another battle for freedom in Lincolnshire.

The land near St. Ives, where Cromwell then had a farm, was very wet and boggy. When drained it made good farming land, so the King's Ministers proposed to spend public money on draining it. This was a good thing to do, except that they then intended to give the good farming land to the Bedford family, who were friends of the King.

The people living around St. Ives were very angry about this, and Cromwell arranged a great meeting against it at Huntingdon.

Cromwell was becoming more and more troubled about the way in which England was being ruled by the King. Many other Englishmen felt the same, and hundreds of them were emigrating to find freedom in the new colonies in America. It is recorded that Cromwell and his cousin Hampden also thought of going, and were actually boarding a ship when they were stopped by an order from the King.

After eleven years, during which the King had governed the country as he pleased, he found that even the illegal taxes did not bring in enough money. So he was forced again to summon a Parliament.

When the members met at Westminster, they were even more determined than before not to grant the King any money unless he agreed to rule according to the advice of Ministers appointed by Parliament. They even arrested one of the King's Ministers and condemned him to death.

King Charles was a very stupid man. When he heard what Parliament had done, he went there with his soldiers to arrest five of the members. But they learned that he was coming, and were gone when he arrived. The King looked round the House of Commons. "I see," he said, "all the birds are flown."

The King returned to his palace determined to get his own way by force. But the members of Parliament were equally angry. War between the King and the Parliament was now certain.

The King and Parliament each now started to recruit an army, and soon the people of England were divided into those who were ready to fight for the King, and those who were determined that the country should be governed by their representatives in Parliament. Those on the side of the King lived mainly in the north and west parts of the country, and those supporting the Parliament were in the east and south-east.

Cromwell returned to Lincolnshire and gathered together a troop of sixty mounted soldiers. With these he rode to Cambridge and seized the castle. In it were a lot of gold and silver articles which were to have been sold to help the King.

In the meantime the King gathered his army at Nottingham and started to march towards London.

Cromwell and his troop joined the Parliament army under the Earl of Essex, and when the two armies met at a place called Edgehill in Warwickshire, his men stood firm when many of the other soldiers ran away. This was because Cromwell was a very stern officer and his soldiers were well trained.

It is strange to us to-day to think of Englishmen fighting and killing each other in the towns and over the fields of England. This is what was happening, and wherever the fighting was most severe, Cromwell and his men had a part in it. In one battle Cromwell's horse was shot from under him.

Soon he was put in charge of the whole of Lincolnshire, and part of his duties was to search the houses of those who were on the King's side for weapons and valuables.

One of the suspected Royalists was his own uncle, Sir Oliver Cromwell, at whose house he had often stayed as a boy.

Sir Oliver was a strange old gentleman and does not seem to have minded having his house searched by his nephew's soldiers. They talked pleasantly together, and when the soldiers left, taking with them guns, ammunition, and furnishings, Sir Oliver gave his nephew his blessing. This was not the only time when Cromwell found himself opposed to his relatives, some of whom were on one side, some on the other.

The men who were on the side of the King were mostly rich men who were afraid that if the Parliament side won, their lands and possessions would be taken away from them. In those days, when horses and carriages were the only means of getting about, these men had many horses and were all used to riding them. So the King's side had a great many mounted soldiers, which were called cavalry.

Because of this, those who followed the King came to be known as Cavaliers.

The foot soldiers of the seventeenth century had not got the weapons to stand up to a charge by soldiers on horseback. Prince Rupert, the King's nephew, commanded the Royalist cavalry and often charged right through the Parliament army of foot soldiers.

So Cromwell and Hampden decided after the battle of Edgehill, that they must have more mounted soldiers to fight Prince Rupert's cavalry. Cromwell immediately set to work to raise more troops of horse soldiers. These men were known as the New Model Army. They soon earned another name for themselves.

The two armies, each consisting of about twenty thousand men, remained for a while in different parts of England, without meeting in a pitched battle. At the same time, fighting between small parties of men was happening all over the country. Sometimes it was one little market town against another; sometimes a party of Roundheads besieging the house of some local Cavalier.

Meanwhile the King and Parliament were sending messages to one another to try to arrange peace. This was difficult because the Parliament men soon found that the King was not to be trusted. He was ready to promise anything, but if he had got back into power he would never have kept his word.

After one battle a lot of the King's private papers and letters were captured. When the Parliament generals read them they found that all the time the King had been deceiving them.

Then came the battle of Marston Moor. It was after this battle that Prince Rupert said Cromwell's horsemen must have iron sides. So "Ironsides" was the name by which they came to be generally known.

The battle of Marston Moor was fought near York on a day in July, 1644. The result was a disaster for the King's forces, led by Prince Rupert.

The Parliament army had been joined by some Scottish soldiers and was drawn up on a hillside overlooking the moor. Cromwell, with his mounted soldiers, was on the left.

Prince Rupert marched out from York to meet them and drew up his men on the moor below the Parliament army. The two armies were quite close to one another, and before Prince Rupert's soldiers were in their positions for the battle, the Parliament soldiers charged down the hill.

At first it looked as though the Parliament army was going to be beaten. The Cavaliers on the right scattered the Scots and thinking that the battle was won, rode after them as they ran away. This left Prince Rupert's horsemen facing Cromwell's Ironsides. After a long and fierce struggle, Cromwell's well trained soldiers were too much for the brave, but undisciplined Cavaliers. Soon they were driven from the field and the battle was won.

Many brave Englishmen were killed on both sides at the battle of Marston Moor. Prince Rupert, who had marched out of York with twenty thousand men, only had six thousand left when he retreated to Oxford.

Cromwell was now a Lieutenant-General, which meant that he commanded a very large number of men. The people on the Parliament side had seen what a good officer he was, and later he was put in command of the whole Parliament army.

The war was now mostly fought in the south and west of England, and the battle of Naseby, in Northamptonshire, in 1645, made victory certain for the Roundheads. The King's soldiers were beaten everywhere, and when Cromwell besieged Oxford, the King knew that he had lost.

So one night, disguised as a servant, he slipped through the Parliament army. The King had hoped to reach the coast and find a ship to take him to Scotland, but all the coasts were well guarded by Cromwell's soldiers. He finally reached Newark, which was held for him by a Scottish army. Here for a time the King was safe.

Soon the Scots found, as Parliament had found before them, that Charles was not to be trusted. They offered to restore him to the throne of England if he would promise to make the English Church like the Church of Scotland, in which there were no bishops. Charles promised, but when they found that he was trying to get French soldiers to fight against them, the Scots realised that he would never keep his word to them.

On January 30th, 1647, the Scots sold the King to the English Parliament for four hundred thousand pounds.

The Parliament kept Charles in a place called Holmby House. But soon quarrels broke out between Parliament and the Roundheads, and Cromwell decided that it would be better that the King should be held by him and his soldiers.

At midnight an officer named Joyce rode to Holmby House with a troop of Cromwell's Ironsides and demanded the surrender of the King. When the Parliament guards asked by what authority he made such a request, he drew his pistol and said, "By this!" There was no further argument.

Parliament was very angry when they heard what Cromwell had done and ordered his arrest. As Cromwell was with the army, which was now as much against the Parliament as it had been against the King, there was no one to carry out the order. In fact things happened the other way about. Cromwell marched to London with the army behind him and expelled many of the members from the House of Commons.

Cromwell was a wise man. He realised that England needed a King, but a King who would rule according to the will of the people. He hoped to make Charles see reason.

Then news came that Charles had again escaped and taken refuge in the Isle of Wight.

Cromwell still hoped to restore the King to the throne as what is called a Constitutional Monarch, which means that laws are made by Parliament and not by the King. He had many long talks with Charles, but when he found that he was still plotting with the Scots and the French, he realised that it was hopeless.

At last even Cromwell recognised the fact that whatever promise Charles made would never be kept. He agreed with the remaining members of Parliament; the King must be held guilty of all the evils which had fallen upon England as a result of his misrule.

On January 20th, 1649, King Charles was brought before a court of justice at Westminster, charged as a tyrant and as one who had caused the death of thousands of Englishmen in the Civil War. He was found guilty, and ten days later, when the palace courtyard at Whitehall was deep in snow, he was executed.

Cromwell tried his best to save the King's life. Charles might have remained on the throne if he had not been as stupid and obstinate as he was untrustworthy.

The King was dead, but the Scots, and many people in England, recognised his son as the rightful King of England. He was crowned in Scotland, and in another book of this series you can read of his adventures before he returned to England, in the year 1660, as King Charles II.

The question was now, who was to rule England? Only fifty-six members remained in Parliament, and very soon they began to quarrel amongst themselves. Cromwell quickly saw that they would never agree long enough to pass the laws necessary to repair the damage of the war.

Cromwell now found himself obliged to do what King Charles had done eleven years earlier: he went to the House of Commons with a regiment of soldiers at his back. But where Charles had failed, Cromwell succeeded.

Marching into the Chamber he cried, "It is not fit that you should sit here any longer. Get you gone and give place to honest men!"

The members were driven out by the soldiers, and the mace, the symbol of the authority of Parliament, was removed. Cromwell locked the doors and put the key in his pocket. When he and the soldiers had gone, a paper was found nailed to the door of the House of Commons. On it was written, "This House to let, unfurnished." It was true. Cromwell was now the supreme ruler of England.

Cromwell did not wish to be what we call a Dictator. He believed that a country ought to be governed by a Parliament chosen by the people. Twice he had a Parliament elected, but as neither agreed with his way of governing England, each was dissolved after only a few months.

It was the second Parliament which offered Cromwell the throne. If he had accepted it, he would have been King Oliver I, which sounds very strange to us. He refused. He knew that as Lord Protector he had much more power than a King.

During all this time England was really ruled by the army. Cromwell was hated by all those who had fought for King Charles, and disliked by those who had later been on the side of the Parliament against the Army.

England was at this time at war with Spain, and Admiral Blake, one of the greatest of English seamen, totally destroyed a Spanish fleet off Teneriffe. By this victory, and by capturing Jamaica from the Spaniards, Cromwell made England respected by all the nations of Europe.

England was well governed while Cromwell was Lord Protector. But for hundreds of years, ever since the time of King John and Magna Carta in 1215, the people of England had been fighting for their rights as free men.

One of these, and the most important, was the right of the people to govern themselves. They now felt that this right had been taken away from them. However well Cromwell ruled, his word was law: the people had no say in the matter.

In Ireland, Cromwell was the most hated of all. There were still men in Ireland who were ready to fight for King Charles II after Charles I had been executed. In order to crush them Cromwell crossed to Ireland with an army.

The Irish were no match for trained and experienced soldiers. The two towns of Drogheda and Wexford, which tried to hold out against them, were besieged and quickly captured. All the defenders were killed without mercy. To this day the people of Ireland hate Cromwell's memory. They have never forgotten Drogheda and Wexford.

Oliver Cromwell was a brave man, as well as being a great one. He had always charged with his men in the battles of the Civil War. Now, with many enemies who wished nothing better than to kill him, he moved freely about the country. He believed always that God would protect him.

Attempts were made to assassinate him. They always failed, and their failure strengthened Cromwell in his faith. God had work for him to do, and it must be fulfilled.

Cromwell was also a good man. He was deeply religious, and neither greedy nor—except in Ireland—cruel. He was a good father to his children and the friend of all honest men.

It is a blot on the history of our country that when Charles II returned, Cromwell's body was taken from the tomb and his head set upon a pike for all to see. It was a mean and unworthy revenge on the part of those whom he had beaten in a fair fight, whose country he had preserved from tyranny, and whose freedom he had ensured.

Cavalier and Lady

Riding Pillion

King Charles' Spaniel

Cromwell's House at Ely

A Countrywoman going to market

A Yorkshire Armchair